Yuck, a Love Story

Don Gillmor · Marie~Louise Gay

Stoddart
Kids
Toronto · New York

For Sophia, Samantha, and Ches
— D.G.

Austin Grouper had a brown dog named Fresco,
a best friend named Sternberg, and a red bicycle.
His life was full.

One day, a new family moved in next door.
"They have a girl who's your age,"
Austin's mother said.
"Her name is Amy."
"Yuck," Austin said.
"Why don't you go over
and welcome her to the neighborhood,"
Mrs. Grouper said.
Austin walked over and knocked on their door.
Amy answered.
She had curly blonde hair and freckles on her nose.
Her shoes had small bows on them.

"The Tyrannosaurus rex
has fifty teeth,"
Austin told her.
"It is the most feared
predator on earth."

"My name is Amy,"
Amy said.

"It mostly eats girls with freckles,"
Austin added,
and went back to his house.
He phoned his friend, Sternberg.
"A girl moved in next door," Austin told him.
"She doesn't know *anything*."

The next day Austin dressed up as his favorite superhero,
Impossible Man. He went over to Amy's house and tried to use
his X-ray vision to see through her front door. He stood there
for two hours, then finally rang the bell. Amy answered.
"I can see through doors and walls with my X-ray
vision," Austin said.
"That's impossible," Amy said.
"That's why I'm called Impossible Man," Austin said,
and went home.
Why did girls have to live next door to *him*? he thought.
Why did they have to live anywhere?

Three days went by. Then Austin built a life-sized statue
of an Apatosaurus out of Popsicle sticks in Amy's yard.
It was bigger than her house.
Amy came out and stared up at it.
"Dinosaurs had very small brains," Amy said.
She was wearing a blue sweater with horses on it.
"So do you," Austin told her, and went home.

Austin's friend, Sternberg, came over.
"She's yucky," Austin told him.
"Who is?" Sternberg asked.
"*Amy*," Austin said. "Amy, Amy, Amy."
After Sternberg left, Austin
stared at the moon, which looked
like it was made out of cheese.

The next day, a card came in the mail.
It was an invitation to Amy's party.
"Isn't that nice!" Austin's mother said.
"Yuck," Austin said.

The night before Amy's birthday, Austin dressed up as a cowboy
and went out into his yard with a very, very long rope.
The moon was as round as a plum.
He was going to lasso it and give it to Amy for her birthday.
He twirled the rope around his head and threw it as high as he could.
It came down and landed on Fresco.
After three hours, he snagged a seagull.

He twirled the rope around his head one more time
and threw it as high and as far as he could.
It settled around the bright white moon. He pulled,
but the moon was heavier than he thought.
It bobbed at the end of the rope
like a huge, helium-filled balloon.
Austin struggled with it and staggered out
of the yard and bounced down the street,
still holding the rope.

As he tried to pull the moon closer, the rope got hooked on a truck heading east. By the time Austin unhooked himself, he was out in farm country, still wrestling with the moon, leaping through a field, trying to avoid the cows.

Then the rope caught
    on a train heading south
and Austin was halfway to Mexico before he wriggled free.
He pulled the moon a little closer and it snagged an airplane flying west.

Then he dropped onto a boat sailing north.
By the time he got back home,
Austin had been to twenty-two countries.
A polar bear had eaten part of the moon in the Arctic.
It was a bit soggy and there was a dent on
one side, but Austin had the moon back
just in time for Amy's party.
He tied it to a tree in her yard
and went in.

He watched Amy open all her presents.
She got a book and a bike and a hamster.
Austin told Amy that his present to her was outside.
She went out with him.
Her birthday dress was red and it shimmered slightly when she walked.

"Thank you, Austin," she said when she saw the moon.
"It's awfully . . . *big*."
"It's the *moon*," Austin said. "It only comes in one size."
The moon, it turned out, *was* made of cheese. Blue cheese.
It didn't smell so great, actually.

Amy broke off a piece and tasted it.
"Yuck," she said.
She offered a piece to Austin who tasted it.
"Yuck," he said.
"Let's go eat some cake, Austin," she said.

And they did.